FREE FALL

FOR KIM

Thanks to Matthew and Daniel

Library of Congress Cataloging-in-Publication Data
Wiesner, David.
Free fall.
Summary: A young boy dreams of daring adventures in the company
of imaginary creatures inspired by the things surrounding his bed.
[1. Dreams—Fiction. 2. Stories without words.] Title.
PZ7.W6367Fr   1988   [E]   87-22834
ISBN 978-0-06-156741-4 (trade bdg.) 978-0-688-05584-4 (library bdg.)
978-0-688-10990-5 (pbk.)

Visit us on the World Wide Web!

www.harpercollinschildrens.com

DAVID WIESNER

FREE FALL

HARPERCOLLINS*PUBLISHERS*

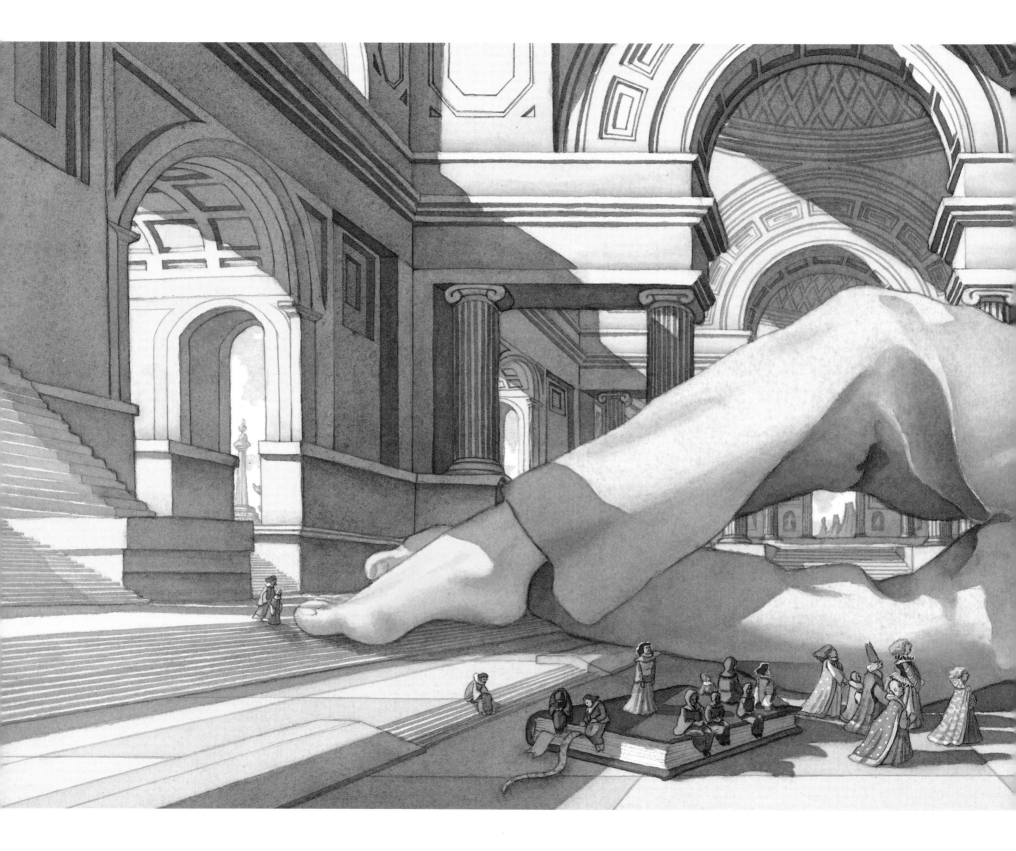